For Evie, may all your adventures
be thrilling! x – T. C.

For Olive x – T. N.

STRIPES PUBLISHING LIMITED
An imprint of the Little Tiger Group
1 Coda Studios, 189 Munster Road,
London SW6 6AW

Imported into the EEA by Penguin Random House Ireland,
Morrison Chambers, 32 Nassau Street, Dublin D02 YH68

www.littletiger.co.uk

A paperback original
First published in Great Britain in 2022

Text copyright © Tracey Corderoy, 2022
Illustrations copyright © Tony Neal, 2022

ISBN: 978-1-78895-326-9

Printed and bound in the UK.

2 4 6 8 10 9 7 5 3 1

THE STORY SHOP

ANCHORS AWAY!

TRACEY CORDEROY
TONY NEAL

LITTLE TIGER
LONDON

WARNING!

Contains weevils, cheats and seagull poop!

Contents

Welcome to Puddletown High Street!

Looks completely normal, doesn't it?

Normal baker's selling normal bread.

Normal shoe shop selling normal wellies.

Normal toyshop selling normal bats and balls.

But nestled between the hairdresser's and the hardware store (which sells *entirely* normal brooms) is the most unusual shop:

The Story Shop sells adventures you can BE in. With real characters you'll *actually* meet!

Shopkeeper Wilbur and his assistant Fred Ferret have props and plots galore.

So, what are you waiting for? Step inside
if you're **BRAVE** enough.

But be warned, *anything* might
happen...

"**Wilbur** – watch!" cried Fred.

It was the end of the day and Fred and Wilbur were tidying the Story Shop.

Fred picked up three hats from the counter, juggled them in the air, then flung them on to the hat stand one by one.

"Hoopla!" chuckled Wilbur.

They did a final check around. Not a costume or prop out of place. But as Fred went to lock the door, a last-minute customer bustled in.

"Your blackboard sign – on the pavement," she tutted. "I **very** nearly tripped over it. I'm Pearl Johnson, famous explorer. I expect you've heard of me?"

They hadn't. But Pearl Johnson *did* look like an explorer. Her trousers were tucked into her well-worn boots and her shirt had lots of pockets. Attached to her belt was a flask and a compass. And dangling around her neck were a pair of binoculars.

"Sorry about the blackboard," Wilbur replied.

"You should have used your binoculars!" joked Fred.

"Actually I was." Pearl examined him closely. "To search for rare birds. On shop rooftops! I had it all planned. Because PLANS," she nodded, "make everything run smoothly."

Fred blushed.

"You need a plan for that sign! If it was MƳ shop," sniffed Pearl, "I'd pop it nearer the wall. I never nearly trip. Though I've been on many **exciting** trips. Why, I was flying planes across the world before you were even born!"

Pearl turned to go, nearly tripping over the doormat. "Honestly," she bristled. "If I were you I'd put that on the planning list too!"

"Very helpful advice," Wilbur nodded. "I wonder if, before we close, you'd like a quick story adventure? We've many thrilling, um ... trips on offer here."

Pearl shrugged. "I challenge you to find something I've not already done. I've crossed deserts, wrestled tigers, sky-dived – blindfolded. I've **even** taken tea with pandas."

"Challenge accepted!" Wilbur replied. And off he went, picking out costumes and props.

He held up some ideas Pearl could 'try for size' – but...

"Done **mummies!**" she declared. "Busted **ghosts** galore."

"And as for p—" Pearl stopped.

"Ever been treasure hunting with pirates?" grinned Fred.

"G-goodness," gasped Pearl. "I haven't!"

Fred hurried behind the counter to pop on his costume, as Wilbur escorted Pearl to the changing room.

When she came back out...

"Look!" she cried.

"I'm a pesky pirate!"

Wilbur laughed. "So you are!"

"Captain Pearl has a rather nice ring to it, don't you think?" She swished her cutlass as Pirate Fred reappeared, sliding his eyepatch into place.

Pearl frowned. "Sorry, but you can't come. I always travel alone."

"But Fred goes on every adventure," insisted Wilbur. "Although," he added hastily, "you'd be in charge as you're so—"

"Bossy," whispered Fred.

"H-helpful!" spluttered Wilbur. "Now let's get your adventure started!"

He whisked the feather off his hat and waved it over a patch of bare floorboards. They parted – **SWISH!** – and up rose a big black pot.

"This is the Story Pot," Fred told Pearl. An inky-blue liquid bubbled inside it.

On a nearby shelf a blank book gave a jiggle, as if **itching** to get the story started. Fred popped it in the pot and Wilbur added a few props...

"A dash of cannon ball. A pinch of crab. And a sprinkle of sand, salt and jewels!"

"And look!" Fred pointed to some drawers behind the counter as one labelled 'Pirates' rattled open.

"Edie!" laughed Wilbur. "Why, of course, *all* pirate captains need a **parrot.**"

The scruffy bird took flight immediately, sending props, books and inkpots flying. She crash-landed on Pearl's arm, a pair of bloomers on her head.

"**Knickers!**"
Edie squawked.

"**Manners!**" sniffed Pearl as Edie shook off the bloomers, a cheeky glint in her eyes.

Wilbur handed Fred a bag of marbles, a torch and two nets to stash in his loot sack.

"Marbles?" said Pearl. "We'll have no time for games when we're running amok with pirates!"

"But these are emergency items," replied Fred. "To help with tricky story twists."

Next Wilbur handed him a toy pirate ship, which Fred slipped into his pocket. Then, taking the spoon, he started to stir.

"Not like **that!**" huffed Pearl, reaching out to grab it. But when *she* touched it too—

WHOOSH! a whirl of bubbles shot from the pot and whizzed off around the shop. They bounced off books and pinged off props, brewing a thrills-and-spills adventure.

"Ooo-argh!" chuckled Wilbur as the bubbles went

POP!

And Fred and Captain Pearl were gone.

THUNK!

They landed behind some barrels and Fred popped up to take a look.

There were cannons. And ropes. And fluttering up a mast was a huge Jolly Roger flag.

"We're on a **real** pirate ship!" gasped Fred.

"Get **down** then!" hissed Pearl. "First we need a *plan*. I didn't wrestle tigers without a plan!"

Fred ducked back down.

"**Nincompoop!**" squawked Edie from her perch on Pearl's shoulder.

"And you can be quiet too!" commanded Pearl, clearly used to doing things *her* way...

"Just ... reporting," whispered Fred, "there are no pirates on deck."

"Then they'll be down *below* it," nodded Pearl. "So, the *plan*: we surprise them, take charge of this ship, and command them to sail us to an island to dig for treasure. Then we'll double-cross them and scarper with **ALL THE LOOT!**"

Fred frowned. "But
what if they don't *want* to?"

"As if they have a choice!"
said Pearl with a nod. "It's my way or walk
the plank!"

She strode from behind the barrels, Edie
gripping on tight and Fred bringing up the
rear.

"To the stairs!" Pearl pointed. "And
mind the rats and weevils."

"But there *are* no rats and weevils?"
shrugged Fred, looking around.

He was right. In fact, the
deck had been swabbed, the
cannons polished, and the
flag's rips neatly mended.
"There's even a
washing line!"
grumbled Pearl.

"Poo pants!" squawked Edie.

"More like *clean* pants," tutted Pearl, noticing a string of underpants blowing in the breeze.

"**This**," said Pearl, rounding on Fred, "is not the adventure I signed up for! You and that **shopkeeper** led me to believe there'd be proper pirates with proper pirate ways!"

Fred gulped. "I ... wait – what's that smell?"

They sniffed the air and Edie coughed. It was **flowery** and coming from below deck.

"It's time," rumbled Pearl, "to find out what's going on!"

They followed the smell down the stairs and along a corridor to a door. Behind the door they could hear voices.

"Careful," said Fred. "It might be a trap."

"I jolly well hope so!" And whipping out her cutlass, Pearl burst through the door yelling: "Rahhhhhhhhhhhhhhh!"

"Arghhhhhhhhhhhhhhh!" came the pirates' terrified reply.

Fred and Edie gaped, eyes wide.

"What on earth—?!" Pearl stopped. This was all wrong.

There were pirates knitting scarves. Pirates arranging flowers. Pirates making mobiles – **out of shells!**

"Please don't hurt us!" they all cried.

"Where's your captain?" demanded Pearl.

"Um ... h-here."

A freshly shaven man shuffled forward in **disgustingly** clean clothes and gleaming boots. He smiled nervously. And in his hand was ... a rose.

Fred wrinkled his nose. "So **that's** the horrid flowery smell."

"I'm Captain Colin," blushed the captain. "How d'you do?"

"**NOT** very well!" bristled Pearl. "Call **yourselves pirates?** My cat Tibbles is scarier! Why aren't you out looking for trouble?!"

"Ah, well," replied the captain. "All pirates are different. And us on the *Pretty Polly* are a friendly bunch who like a spot of crafting on a Tuesday."

"But it's *Wednesday!*" snapped Pearl.

"Ooo-argh!" the captain nodded. "And **normally** we'd be fishing today, except we didn't finish our crafting yesterday."

He shuffled nervously. "And, er, who might you be?"

"Captain Pearl!" snapped Pearl. "And this is Pirate ... Fredrick and my rascally parrot Edie."

"Fred," nodded Fred, and Edie blew the pirates a raspberry.

"Now then," sniffed Pearl. "I'm here for a **proper** pirate adventure, which is why I'm taking over your ship!"

"**Nooooo!**" wailed the pirates.

Fred saw their look of fear and quickly stepped forward.

"Don't panic! I'm sure we can come to some arrangement to keep everyone happy," he said.

He turned to the captain. "Any battles brewing? O-or pressing pirate problems ... big or small?"

"Well, we **did** have a problem," Captain Colin replied. "We dug up some treasure. An **enormous** black pearl. Jake Smallsparrow found it one Daytrip Friday."

"**Ooo**-argh!" Jake waved his knitting at them with a grin.

"But then Captain GRIME pinched it off us," sighed the captain.

"Then go and get it back!" boomed Pearl.

"Can't," shrugged the captain. "We don't

stand a *chance* against the *Scabby Seagull* crew. They're bigger and badder and sneakier than us."

"Plus," gulped Roger Roundfellow, "some say they don't EVEN ... *wash their underwear!*"

Fred knew what was coming...

"THANK GOODNESS!" roared Pearl, and Edie almost jumped out of her feathers. "A proper pirate adventure. And of course, I have a PLAN!"

She turned to the crew. "I shall teach you to be SNEAKIER. Then we're off to steal back your black pearl!"

"Right!" said Pearl. "Time to learn to be SNEAKY." She'd set up a barrel assault course on deck. "To teach you how to dodge," she explained.

She stood at one end and Fred stood at the other, while the pirates wove in and out of the barrels. If they bumped into any, Edie sent them back to the start by blowing a giant raspberry.

Poor Roger Roundfellow was back and forth like a yo-yo!

Next, they had to sneak up the rigging – **unseen.**

"LOOK at ME!"

yelled Timid Thomas.

"I is sneaking right **FAST.**"

"Shhh!" roared the others.

"Ooops! Right. S-sorry," Thomas whispered.

Finally, they set tripwires using spare balls of wool. Everyone got the hang of this except Jake...

"We do NOT," said Pearl, unravelling a dangling sock, "*knit* the tripwire!"

When everyone had passed the Sneakier-than-Sneaky Test Fred dished out certificates and badges.

"Now we just need a thick mist," whispered Pearl, "so we can swarm aboard the *Scabby Seagull* unseen."

"*Swarm* aboard?" Captain Colin gulped. "We might be sneaky, but we're STILL not brave. Eeek!"

When the mist was a right peasouper, Pearl assembled her crew.

"What's this now?" she gasped as they appeared up on deck.

"D-disguises," stuttered Captain Colin. "They make us feel braver. Plus, Grime's lot won't know it's US – sneaky, eh?!"

Captain Colin was a crab, Jake a jellyfish and Pirates Pete, Paul and Patrick were prawns. The rest of the crew were glo-stick eels.

"We would have been *electric* ones," Roger Roundfellow said. "But we had some spare glo sticks in the craft box."

Pearl sighed. "How on **earth** do you dodge in *tentacles*? And climb rigging – sneakily – in fish heads?"

But there was no time to argue – a prawn had raised the anchor – so off they went.

The journey was bumpy. And windy. And wet. Just the sort of trip Pearl liked!

Finally, Edie let out a cheeky—

"Knickers!"

"Enemy ship ahoy!" Jake called from his perch in the crow's nest.

They dropped anchor and everyone peered across at the *Scabby Seagull*.

"Singing!" whispered Pearl. It was coming from below deck, along with the scraping of cutlery.

"They're having supper," said Fred.

"To the ropes then!" commanded Pearl. "Follow my lead!"

She swung across, followed by Fred, then the terrified crew of the *Pretty Polly*. But although Pearl had taught them to be sneaky and brave-*ish* – nothing could prepare them for...

...this!

"Weevils in the b-biscuits!" Captain Colin shuddered.

"Rats up the rigging!" jiggled Jake.

"And NO washing line!" gulped Roger. "So, they DON'T wash their underwear! They're MONSTERS!"

"Shhhh!" hissed Pearl. "Remember the plan. Get searching – and stay sneaky!"

"Aye aye, Captain Pearl!" said the crew.

The glo-stick eels checked loose floorboards for secret hidey-holes, while Captain Colin used his crab claws to poke under the ropes. The prawns peeped down cannons and Jake drained the barrels as Fred and Edie kept lookout by the galley door. As they searched, Captain Pearl strode around whispering commands and dodging mountains of seagull poop!

After ten minutes of searching, they were still empty-handed and the singing below deck had just stopped.

"The treasure," whispered Pearl, "must be down with Captain Grime."

"Ah," Captain Colin shrugged. "Best get back to our ship then."

"Not so fast!" hissed Pearl.
"I never give—"

"Argggh!" Fred let out
a shriek.

They all spun round to
see him gripped in the
fist of Captain Grime.

4

"Poo!" squawked Edie, holding her beak. Captain Grime smelled like a **drain.**

The crew of the *Scabby Seagull* sniggered.

"Well!" Grime guffawed, flashing a mouth full of mouldy teeth. "If it ain't the *Pretty Polly* crew! As *if* you'd fool **us** in them disguises."

Then suddenly he noticed Pearl. "And who be **you?**"

"Captain Pearl!" She glared. "Now

unhand Pirate Fredrick and return what you pinched from Captain Colin and his crew – the black pearl!"

Captain Grime leaned forward, a stray rat in his beard twitchily watching the action. "Make me!" grunted Grime.

"Pleasure!" grinned Pearl. She spun to face her crew.

"Attack!"

The *Pretty Polly* crew tried really hard, but it was no good. They got tangled in their tentacles and tripped over their tails. Then the glo-stick eels went and

POPPED!

Before they knew it, the crew of the *Pretty Polly* were tied to the mast.

"But not for long!" snorted Captain Grime, striding across to the cannons.

Fred gulped. "They're going to FIRE us back to our ship!"

"NOT," hissed Pearl, "until we get that treasure back. We just need to be sneakier!"

"How on earth—" But Fred stopped. He'd just had a *marble-ous* idea!

While the baddies busied themselves with the cannons, Fred put Edie to work pecking through the ropes to free the crew.

When she'd nibbled the last knot, Fred edged his hand into his loot sack and took out the bag of marbles Wilbur had given him.

"What are you up to?" Pearl frowned.

"I just thought," whispered Fred, "when Grime's lot come for us, we could scatter these marbles and they'd—"

"Slip on them. Yes! I thought that too!" cut in Pearl. "Buying us time to … swarm below deck and finish our hunt for the pearl."

"No! Time to swarm to the *ropes* and escape in one piece!" gasped Fred.

"Oi! What are you two arguing about?" Captain Grime called over. He snatched up his telescope to take a closer look but stopped sharp and slipped it back into his belt.

"Eh?" muttered Fred.

But then he saw why. The telescope had no lens. Because hidden inside was the black pearl!

"I just saw—" But Fred stopped. He'd never hear the end of it unless Pearl thought she'd found the treasure.

"Um, if I was hiding treasure," hinted Fred, "I'd put it somewhere I could keep a close eye on it."

"Obviously," sniffed Pearl. "Like a pocket. Or down a sock."

"Or somewhere I could see it," said Fred.

Pearl stared over at Captain Grime and gasped.

"The black pearl!" she whispered. "It's in his telescope. I found it!"

The rest happened quickly. As the crew of the *Scabby Seagull* approached, Fred shot the marbles across the deck.

"Treasure!" he shouted. "Wondrous, stripy pearls!"

"WHAT?!" Grime's lot dashed after them, slipping and sliding all over the place.

They bashed into barrels – **BANG!**
THWACK!
They clattered into cannons
– **KERRR-DOIN-NG-GG!**
As Grime and his crew landed in a
heap, the telescope flew from his belt.
Pearl dived for it but – "Bother!" – she
tripped over her bootlace and Jake caught
it – by accident – instead.

"Oo-er!" In panic, he chucked it to Thomas, who "Arghhhh!" sent it spinning to Roger.

"No!" Roger lobbed it high into the air, where Edie snatched it in her beak and dropped it **right on target...**

"Look what *I* caught!" cried Pearl, as it landed in her hands.

"To the ropes!" gulped Fred. "On the double!" The Scabby Seagulls were back on their feet!

The *Pretty Polly* crew swiftly swung back to their ship. Then Pearl handed over the telescope.

Captain Colin scooped out the black pearl and beamed.

"Thank you!" he and his shipmates cried. It was just as awesome as they remembered.

"It was nothing!" tittered Pearl. "Just another successful plan under my belt."

It was time to go, and Pearl had it all planned. She and Fred jumped into two empty barrels which they rolled down the plank and—

SPLASH!

Then off they bobbed to their next
adventure, Edie flapping chirpily behind.

Race to the Treasure!

Pearl and Fred bobbed about in their barrels for what felt like hours. Then, just as they were getting hungry...

"Land ahoy!" cried Fred.

Pearl peered across to some sunny desert islands. "Oh! And look," she smiled. A Jolly Roger flag fluttered in the sand. "More pirates!"

They sailed over, Edie fluttering above. But just as their barrels washed up on shore...

FWIP! – a fishing net flew through the air capturing them like kippers.

"Uh-oh..." Fred gulped, but Pearl's eyes twinkled.

"How thrilling!"

A bunch of terrifying pirates stepped out from behind a big rock. They looked rough, unwashed and very mean.

"Well, what have we 'ere?" grinned the scariest-looking one. "Looks like a couple of SPIES!"

"Nonsense!" cried Pearl. "Now un-net us at—"

"OI!" the scary pirate glared back. "Only Long Jane Silver gives commands around 'ere – and that's ME!"

"**Knickers!**" squawked Edie, eyeing up the pirate captain.

"Shhh!" Fred nudged her. But luckily Long Jane Silver hadn't heard.

She clicked her fingers. "Moldy Maud! Sweaty Betty! Take these spies to the cave!"

Two pirates stepped forward, slashed the net with their cutlasses and plucked Pearl and Fred from inside. Moldy Maud had a face full of boils and Sweaty Betty dripped sweat like a leaky tap.

"There's no need to prod!" piped up Pearl as they were marched into a nearby cave. It was damp and dimly lit with lanterns.

"Arggh!" Pearl tripped over a half-built raft. "If this was *my* cave—" she began.

"But it isn't!" rumbled Long Jane Silver.

Pearl and Fred were
prodded to the floor among a
clutter of canvas sheets, ropes and
poles. Maps and plans filled the walls,
hammered in with big iron nails.

"So!" sniffed Pearl. "What makes you think we're spies?"

"Oi – I ask the questions!" boomed Jane. "Because sending spies is just the kind of sneaky stunt Blunderbuss Bob would pull to win the race!"

At his name, the crew rumbled like a swarm of angry bees.

"Never heard of him!" argued Pearl. "And I work for no one but myself. Captain Pearl's the name and this is Pirate Fredrick and my rascally parrot Edie."

Fred nodded and Edie went to blow a raspberry but changed her mind.

"So, this um ... Blunderbuss ... Bob," said Fred, trying not to make it sound like a question.

"Our number one enemy in the race!" hissed Jane. "So – IF you're not his spies,

what are you doing 'ere?"

"Having an adventure," said Pearl. "And a RACE sounds just the ticket! Let us join your crew and—"

"Hang on," gulped Fred.

"And we could help you win!" went on Pearl.

Jane frowned. "How?"

"Spy on Bob for you."

"HA! He'd stomp you into next week!" Jane grinned slyly. "But I ain't got nothing to lose. So ... you're on!"

"No!" shrieked Fred, leaping up. He didn't like the sound of Blunderbuss Bob at all. "S-sorry, but we must be off."

"Off?" frowned Pearl, eyeballing him. "Says who?!" She marched to the wall. "I spy raft plans!"

"Aye, for the race," explained Jane.

"Every year," said Sweaty Betty, "us pirates have a competition ending with a big treasure hunt. It kicks off with three tasks: a raft race to Treasure Island, building a shelter to camp in, and whipping up a delicious supper."

"Each task earns the winning crew ten points," beamed Moldy Maud. "And the crew with the most points by the end of tonight will set off first on the treasure hunt tomorrow morning."

"How thrilling!" cried Pearl and Fred gave a groan. Pearl was hooked!

"First things first!" growled Jane. "Go spy on Bob's raft. Then sneakily **WRECK** it so it'll sink in the race."

"Consider it done!" Pearl whistled for Edie, and swept Fred outside.

"Are you sure about this?" whispered

Fred. "Shouldn't we just escape while we can?"

"I'm certain!" nodded Pearl. "We'll work with Jane until—"

"Until what?" gasped Fred, and Pearl tapped her nose.

"I happen to have a TOP SECRET plan," she whispered. "And when I'm **ready**, Pirate Fredrick, you shall know it. But first, let's go and spy on Bob. What fun!"

Pearl **insisted** they crept over to Bob's cave under a maggoty old rowing boat.

"It stinks!" grumbled Fred, and Edie held her beak.

"Yes, but we need to be **sneaky.**" Pearl winked. "Trust me!"

She parked the boat a little way off. Then they peeped through a couple of holes. Bob's crew were around the side of their cave making their raft.

"Tie them knots tighter," barked big,

burly Bob. "We's gotta beat that Jane."

"**Ooo-argh!!**" chorused his crew,
jumping to it.

When they'd finished, Bob tested the
raft's strength by stomping on it hard.

"Good," he grunted. "Now time for some grub. Let's go."

Pearl waited for the crew to disappear inside the cave then crawled out from under the boat.

"Follow me," she said, creeping over to the raft. "Right, Edie – peck through those knots."

"No, wait!" Fred frowned. "They'll notice that right away. We've got to do something more ... sneaky."

"Put a sock in it!" chirped Edie.

"Edie!" hissed Pearl.

"Hang on," Fred grinned. "I think she's trying to **help.** Look..."

On a nearby rock, the crew's socks were

drying in the sunshine. Edie pecked at one and the wool around the rim started to unravel.

"We'll do a *switch*," grinned Fred. "The raft's strong rope for the socks' much thinner wool. Bob won't know the difference, but it'll snap in the waves."

"Um ... yes!" said Pearl. "That's exactly what I was thinking."

They quickly made the switch, then snuck back to report...

"Oh," grunted Jane. "You're back."

"Indeed!" beamed Pearl. "Raft wrecking DONE. And now I'll help build our raft. So! Viking ships had fierce figureheads and huge sails to scare the enemy..."

"No!" said Jane flatly.

"Yes, yes!" nodded Pearl. "I have a plan!"

At sunset, the crews lined up on the sand. It was time for the raft race to Treasure Island.

Rapscallion Reg (a famous past winner) had come to judge the tasks. He had a sly, pointy face and twirly moustache.

"Ready?" he smirked.

"Well, we are!" snorted Bob. "Not sure about Jane, though."

All the crews started to snigger at her raft. After MUCH bickering, Pearl had got her way. The raft itself was strong and sturdy, but Pearl had added a 'scary Viking figurehead' made out of driftwood and seaweed, which looked more like a scruffy cat than a lion. And her sail was as big as a giant's underpants!

Reg raised his starter flag. "And remember to CHEAT— Oh!"

Bob had already set off.

"After 'im!" roared Jane. And snatching up their rafts, the crews all raced into the waves. Soon they were bashing and crashing like bumper cars.

Move!

Then Jane spied Bob up in front.
"You!" she growled at Pearl. "Were
meant to wreck his raft!"
"We **did!**"
"So, why's it not **sinking?!**"
Fred and Pearl exchanged
puzzled looks. Maybe Bob had
discovered the wool?

"Anyways," boomed Jane,
"less load more speed!" And
whirling her paddle over her
head, she walloped Pearl's
figurehead into the sea.

"**How dare you!**" cried Pearl, waving her paddle at Jane.

"Fight!" beamed Sweaty Betty, and everyone waded in.

Fred shook his head. This was ridiculous. He caught Edie's eye and she gave a shrill "**Peep!**"

"**WHAT?!**" Everyone stopped and glared.

"Listen," cried Fred, quickly starting to paddle. "We can still catch Bob if we work together. **Now!**"

One by one, the others joined in until their raft was going quite fast. Jane's muscles helped, but so did Pearl's huge sail.

They powered through the pack and were just a whisker from Bob, when Moldy Maud gave a shriek—

"His raft's breaking!"

Bob looked down.

"So you are!" grinned Jane, storming past him to the finish line!

"Hooray!" cheered the crew.

"That's the first ten points to us!" beamed Fred.

"Ooo-argh!" cried Jane. She looked rather pleased. But not for very long. As the other crews washed up on shore, she was already thinking about shelters.

"Sweaty Betty – get the canvas," commanded Jane.

"Oh, you won't be needing that," piped up Pearl. "Once on my travels I—"

"No!" said Jane flatly.

"Yes, yes!" nodded Pearl. "I have a plan!"

Pearl insisted she knew **A LOT** about shelters. But Jane was having none of it.

"You," Jane grunted, "are here to SPY ON BOB. So, go and see what his shelter is made of. Then wreck it by making some 'oles."

Pearl protested, but Jane held her ground.

"Right!" huffed Pearl. She gathered Fred and Edie and five minutes later they set off, camouflaged as palm trees.

They planted themselves a safe distance from Bob's camp, then spied through binoculars disguised as coconuts.

"Aha!" said Pearl. "Bob's shelter is canvas. Let's report back to Jane."

"But what about making 'oles?" said Fred.

"Don't need them," smiled Pearl.

"'Oles or not, a canvas shelter will never win this task!"

Uprooting themselves, they shuffled back...

"Oh, you again." Jane's face fell.

"Indeed!" beamed Pearl. "Bob's shelter is canvas, which is totally wrong for this weather!"

"Not if it rains," insisted Jane.

"But there isn't a cloud in the sky," insisted Pearl.

Then Pearl noticed *Jane's* shelter was made of canvas too.

"Good heavens!" she cried, ripping the palm leaves off her costume. "Use these instead. Honestly – it'll be far less sweaty inside."

"NO!" scowled Jane.

"Yes, yes!" insisted Pearl. "Because once, on one of my MANY trips I—"

"OK, OK! Pass them over!" growled Jane.

"But ONLY if you go BACK to Bob's to spy on his supper this time."

"Again?" said Fred. It was almost as if Jane wanted them to get caught.

"Sure!" replied Pearl. "But we'll be needing this..."

And ripping the canvas off Jane's shelter, back they went again – undercover – disguised as wriggly sand worms.

"Clever, eh?" smiled Pearl.

But as they reached Bob's camp – FWIP! – the canvas was whipped away.

"Uh-oh!" squawked Edie. It was Blunderbuss Bob in his big, stompy boots.

"Now what have we 'ere?" he growled. "SPIES? Or 'ave you come to barter?"

"To b-barter ... why, yes!" Pearl held up the canvas. "We have this to swap. And you?"

Bob grinned. "Follow me!"

He marched them into his shelter and picked up a small jar.

"Swap my spice for your canvas?" he said to Pearl. "It's me mum's secret recipe. A right winner!"

Fred frowned and Edie let out a warning squawk, but Pearl's eyes lit up. "Deal!"

Back at camp, Moldy Maud was outside brewing supper over a campfire. Pearl hurried across and tipped Bob's spice into the vile-looking mixture.

"Oi!" yelled Maud.

"Trust me," nodded Pearl, tapping the side of her nose.

She turned to their shelter, now a tangle of leaves – and battled her way in, with Fred and Edie following behind.

"Doh!" rumbled Jane.

"Yes, us again!" beamed Pearl. "Back to report that Blunderbuss Bob isn't half as bad as you made out. In fact, he swapped our useless canvas for a winning ingredient for our supper!"

"Hang on," growled Jane, but the sound of a booming cannon signalled the end of the tasks.

"Time for Reg to judge the shelters and suppers!" beamed Pearl. "Let's go!"

Rapscallion Reg moved along the shelters, inspecting them one by one.

Next, Reg stopped at Jane's shelter.

"Palm leaves?" he tutted.

Jane glowered at Pearl.

"Excuse me," piped up Pearl. "It's *much* more hygienic when *clearly* it's NOT going to rain."

"Err," Fred nudged her, as a raindrop bounced off his nose. Then suddenly...

KATSSSHHHHHHHHHHH!

the heavens opened.

"Ten points to Bob!" cried Reg, wading off to judge the suppers.

"Too salty, Captain Tunabeard!"

"Too lumpy, Captain Bess."

"Too – aaaaachooooooo! – peppery, Captain Poopdeck!"

Then came Bob's 'Fruits of the Sea' pizza.

"Ah, *now* we're talking..." Reg took a big bite.

"Don't forget our stew!" Moldy Maud interrupted, stuffing her ladle into his hand.

"He's going to *love* it," Pearl whispered to Jane. "With that spice Bob gave—"

"Hang on!" hissed Jane. "Don't tell me you actually *used* it?!"

Pearl nodded. "A big *slug* of it, just like Bob said. I—"

"S-slug..." gulped Jane.

"Reg – STOP!" she shrieked. But too

late! Reg had slurped in a mouthful.
Everyone watched as his face
turned green.

"Sea-Slug Spice!"
gulped Reg.
"REVOLTING!
The final ten points go
to Bob!"

"Ha! SUCKERS!" Bob
jeered at Jane. Now *his*
crew would be first to set
off on the Treasure Hunt
in the morning.

As Jane settled to sleep under their
flappy, draughty shelter she did not look
happy at ALL.

"I could just—" Pearl began.

"NO!" roared Jane. "You'll do
nothing!"

Doing nothing, however, was not Pearl's style. It was time for her **TOP SECRET** plan!

Early next morning, when everyone was still asleep, she was up and waiting for the post parrots to deliver maps for the treasure hunt.

Suddenly... **WHOOSH!** A scroll burst through their shelter and Pearl caught it before it hit the ground.

This was it! A proper pirate treasure map!

Grabbing Jane's spade, she prodded Fred and Edie awake.

"Time to get treasure hunting," whispered Pearl. "Let's go..."

She crept outside, Fred shuffling behind.

"But it's cheating!" he yawned.

"Pirates are *meant* to cheat," whispered Pearl.

Her eyes twinkled. "And this," she added, "is my **top secret plan.**"

"OK," grinned Fred. This *was* her adventure after all.

It was dark so Fred slipped his hand into his loot sack and took out the torch Wilbur had given them.

"Now," said Pearl, "we'll need to work fast." At sunrise Bob's crew would be hot on their heels and the others not far behind them.

Finally, at the top of the fifth biggest sand dune, Edie gave a wide-awake "Squawk!"

"What?!" Pearl jumped. Then suddenly she saw it. "Oh, look! I found X marks the spot!"

They hurried down.

"Ah, *but*," Pearl nodded, "I bet this is a trap."

"Eh?" said Fred.

"Trust me!" said Pearl. She walked ten paces right. "I'm digging here!"

Fred frowned. "O-OK." But while she was busy, he and Edie decided to dig on the X. Fred loved digging and was shifting sand at speed when suddenly he hit something solid.

"Captain Pearl!" he called over. "Quick! Here!"

Pearl clambered out of her pit.

"What now? I— Oh!" she gave a gasp.
"A treasure chest!"

Pearl rubbed her hands together. "I'll
take it from here."

Fred handed it over and Pearl opened
the lid. But instead of gold in the chest
there was just an old boot.

"Hey! I *know* this boot,"
muttered Pearl. "It's..."

"Mine!" came a voice from the top of the sand dune and Long Jane Silver hobbled down wearing just *one* boot. Under her arm was a big, sandy treasure chest FULL of gold.

"Just dug it up!" smirked Jane. "I knew you'd try to trick me, so I got a parrot I know to drop you a nice fake map. Then I waited for the *real* map to the treasure, and—"

"OI!"

And who should **now** appear but...

Bob.

"You dirty rotten CHEATS!"

He shook his fists. "I was meant to set off first!"

The air now filled with the rumble of footsteps as Bob's *and* Jane's crews swarmed to battle.

"Time to go!" gasped Fred.

"Good plan!" agreed Pearl.

They jumped down the hole Pearl had dug and Fred began tunnelling at speed.

Pearl hurried after him with Edie right
behind.

"Oh! I wonder where the tunnel will
lead?" beamed Pearl.

She couldn't *wait* to find out!

The Ghost
Pirate

The long, sandy tunnel off Treasure Island led to another beach.

Pearl looked around. "Doh," she frowned. "I was hoping to be on another pirate ship."

Above them seagulls were circling in the sky making Edie dizzy.

Fred sniffed the air. "I smell fish and chips!"

"Never mind that," tutted Pearl. "I want PIRATES."

She marched them up a set of steps to get a better view.

"Aha!"

Fred pointed to some boats in the harbour. In among the neat, shiny ones was a big pirate galleon. Its tattered sails billowed in the breeze.

"That's more like it!" Pearl rubbed her hands together. "But where are the crew? I think it's time to sniff out those pirates!"

With Edie on her shoulder, Pearl strode across the road then up the narrow, cobbled streets. They passed a few shops selling buckets and spades. Then they came to a street of tall houses.

Each one was painted in ice-cream colours – minty green, lemon, strawberry pink, and...

"Black!" gasped Fred.

Beside the door was a flowerpot in the shape of an old cannon, a prickly plant bursting out of it. Pearl marched up and read the sign in the window...

MEG O'CUTTLEFISH GUESTHOUSE FOR PIRATES. (So DON'T BOTHER KNOCKING IF YOU AIN'T ONE!)

"So *that's* where they're hiding!"
She thumped on the door.

BANG! BANG! BANG!

"Wait!" gulped Fred. "We're not real
pirates!"

"Of course we are!" cried Pearl.

"Ooo-argh!" Edie squawked in agreement.

Suddenly, the door was flung open and a
red-faced lady glared out.

"We's full!" she snapped. Her hair was like
candyfloss springing out from under a cook's
hat. She wore a stripy apron and an earring
that looked like a fish fang.

"We just need a *small* room," insisted
Pearl as a crew of fearsome-looking pirates
appeared behind the lady.

"Go on, Meg – let 'em in!" the pirate
captain roared. "Then we can swap
pirating stories!"

Meg sucked her teeth. "Oh, well … fine! You can 'ave the tiny attic room. If the rats don't mind you sharing!"

"Huh! Rats don't scare me…" said Pearl, sweeping Fred and Edie inside.

The dark hallway was full of pirate bits and bobs – old hats, flags, cannon balls and maps.

By the stairs stood a mermaid figurehead that Meg had turned into a coat stand. A parrot clock hung on the wall nearby.

"A-and who are t-they…?" Fred gaped at a row of dusty portraits. Each one was of a dodgy-looking pirate.

"Ah, that's my Ghostly Gallery," Meg explained. "This bunch of rapscallions are known to haunt us pirates – though I've not met any of them yet."

"N-nor me!" the pirate captain spluttered. "Anyways, it's d-draughty out here – move along." Fred wasn't complaining. The ghosts on the wall were terrifying!

Meg led them into the dining room and the pirate captain introduced himself.

"I'm Captain Swashbuckle, and this is me crew, the Goblin Sharks," he said.

"They're big and brave," grinned Meg. "And not scared of **nothing.**"

"Nor are we!" nodded Pearl. "I'm Captain Pearl. And this is Pirate Fredrick and Edie."

Fred nodded – though in truth he did feel a bit scared – and Edie flexed her fluffy muscles.

"Right!" Pearl nudged Meg. "Pop the kettle on, dear. It's time for us pirates to swap stories of derring-do – ooo-argh!"

Half an hour later, Pearl was wolfing down Meg O'Cuttlefish's delicious chocolate brownies. She was also *trying* to tell of her many THRILLING past adventures...

"So *once*," began Pearl. "I fought—"

"Excuse I!" Captain Swashbuckle raised his sword. "Once WE did fight the Kraken – ooo-argh. The most *wicked* of sea monsters there be."

"Um ... marvellous," said Pearl.

"Whereas *I* fought the—"

"Excuse I!" Cutlass Cath raised her many swords. "WE did outsmart the Red Octopus too. Tied her in knots we did!"

"Yes, yes!" puffed Pearl. "Whereas I—" She stopped again as Muscles Marv burst into song...

"*There once-was-a-serpent-called-Big-Tim! He-liked-to-nip-so-we-didn't-like him-then*—"

"Stop!" yelled Pearl. "It's MY turn now."

Fred rolled his eyes. This was turning into a competition.

"Now! Once on *my* travels," Pearl hurried on. "I fought a whole family of monster sea snakes. W-whilst booting away the Kraken's MUCH bigger cousin ... Kevin!"

"Stop fibbing," whispered Fred.
"Or you'll get us into trouble."

"Liar, liar, pants on fire!" snorted Edie.
Pearl stuffed a chocolate brownie in her
beak and continued on with her story!

Two hours later they were STILL at it
when—

"Oi! Pack it in!" Meg called from the
door. "I need to set the table for supper.
I might not be Cook on a pirate ship no
more, but I was once the BEST on the
ocean!"

"Oooo! Why did you leave pirating?"
piped up Pearl, and the Goblin Sharks
leaned in to listen.

"Now that," Meg waved her rolling pin
wildly, "is none of your business. Right!
To the lounge until supper's ready. Crew
dismissed!"

At seven on the dot, the parrot clock in the hall gave seven ear-splitting squawks.

"Supper!" roared Meg.

Pearl led the way. "Come on, Captain Swashbuckle, I'm starving!"

The dining-room table was filled with food. All the pirates' favourites! There was a hearty fish stew, pies shaped like treasure chests, prawn crackers and chips like fat gold bars. Everyone tucked in. Then it was time for...

"Me showstopping trifle!" beamed Meg.
It had sea-blue jelly that teemed
with fish-shaped sweets.

She dished it out and they all dived in.
"Oh, and popping candy!" giggled Fred,
feeling it explode on his tongue.

"I always puts popping candy in," Meg said proudly. "It's me – shhh – **secret ingredient.**"

Meg had the biggest bowlful of all. "Haven't made it for so long," she smiled. "I'd forgotten how good it is!"

After supper it was time to cheat at a few board games, until—

"**Squaw-aaaahhhh...**" The parrot clock yawned loudly.

"Right! Bedtime!" Meg commanded. "Crew dismissed!"

On their way upstairs, Pearl couldn't resist another look at the Ghostly Gallery.

"E-excuse I!" Captain Swashbuckle tried to budge past. "I'll fight the Kraken *blindfolded*," he said. "But g-ghosts give me the s-shivers."

Fred quite agreed. But...

"Nonsense!" laughed Pearl. "Ghost pirates are **thrilling.** Haunting by moonlight – wooOohHh!"

The first portrait was of a skinny pirate with rotten teeth. Pearl read the plaque below. "Jones de Bones."

Next came Captain Hex whose stare made her go a bit dizzy.

She moved along the line, finally stopping at a pirate who was gripping an enormous spade.

111

"That's Spade-at-the-Ready-Neddy!" Meg sucked her teeth. "A right terror when he was alive."

"**Stinker!**" squawked Edie.

"Too right!" Meg nodded. "And *now* he haunts us pirates – **wailing** and **clunking** that spade!"

"**Meg – stop!**" The Goblin Sharks stuffed their fingers in their ears.

"Oh, pull yourselves together! And you," tutted Pearl as Fred nervously chewed his neckerchief.

Meg grinned. She'd had many a pirate at the guesthouse who was scared of ghosts.

Squeezing past, she opened a cupboard door and a bundle of teddies tumbled out.

"Anyone for a cuddly bear?"

"**Me!**" cried the Goblin Sharks.

They each grabbed a bear then scarpered up to bed.

"They left the fluffiest," said Fred.

"Well, now," sniffed Pearl. "You won't be needing that!"

She ushered him and Edie upstairs too and soon they were tucked up in bed.

"Once on my travels, there was a REAL ghost," began Pearl. "And... Oh."

She stopped. Fred and Edie seemed to be fast asleep already.

3

"**Arrrgggh?!**" Fred woke suddenly.

It was pitch-black. But someone – or some*thing* – was wailing.

He switched on his torch. Pearl was fast asleep, as was Edie.

Fred listened, wide-eyed, to the horrible din—

"**Gaaaaahhhaaaaa!**" It was coming from a room below.

It was rattling the windows...

"**Gahhaahhahhh-ghaahhhh!**"

It was bumping the door.

"Gha-hhuhuaaaauH!"

This had to be the sound of a wailing ghost.

"C-C-Captain P-P-Pearl!" Fred whispered, giving her a shake. "Wake up! I can hear s-s-s-something..."

In an instant Pearl was out of bed. "How thrilling!" she whispered. "Follow me!"

They crept outside on to the dusty landing. Fred's torch made the little spiders in the cobwebs look like monsters.

They followed the wailing down the attic stairs and on to the landing below. The Goblin Sharks were there in a huddle, teddies **gripped.**

"It's a g-g-g-ghost!" trembled Captain Swashbuckle, his eyes wide with fear.

"S-Spade-at-the-Ready-N-Neddy!"

gasped Cutlass Cath.

"Nonsense!" replied Pearl. "Neddy wails and clunks. It must be another random spook."

"**A-another one?!**" The pirates gripped their teddies even tighter. "**Noooo!**"

"**QUIET!**" boomed Pearl, and the wailing suddenly stopped.

"**Phew!**" Fred gasped. Pearl's shout had sent the ghost packing!

"What's going on?!" Meg appeared at her bedroom door in rollers and puffer-fish slippers. "Your **bellowing** woke me up!" She glared at Pearl.

"My bellowing?" huffed Pearl. "Didn't you hear the wailing? There was a g—"

"Don't say the 'g' word!" Captain Swashbuckle was trembling.

Meg shook her head. "It was probably
the wind. Now back to bed, the lot of you!"

As everyone trooped back to their rooms,
Pearl gave Meg a nudge.

118

"Don't worry," she whispered. "If there *is* a ghost, then I have a cunning plan."

"Good idea," Meg nodded. "But I'm sure it was absolutely nothing..."

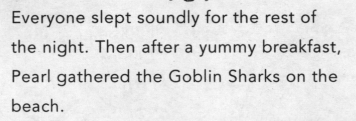

Everyone slept soundly for the rest of the night. Then after a yummy breakfast, Pearl gathered the Goblin Sharks on the beach.

"I have a plan," she announced, "to booby-trap Meg's guesthouse. So if the wailing 'whatever' comes back tonight – me, Fred and Edie will get it!"

"H-hang on!" gulped Fred.

"Now," continued Pearl, "we need to find some good things for booby traps. Chop-chop!"

They scattered and scoured the beach, gathering anything they could find...

That afternoon they worked on their booby traps, carrying on into the night. Meg brought them cheese on toast for supper but kept the leftover trifle for herself!

At ten o'clock the parrot clock yawned, and Meg sent the Goblin Sharks to bed.

"Stay put if you hear any ghosts," Pearl reminded them. "Leave the capture to me and my crew."

"Yep. Sure. We d-definitely will," they nodded.

While Edie kept watch from the banister, Pearl and a very nervous Fred positioned the traps around the house.

A huge, seaweed jellyfish dangled from the landing light to scare off any passing spook. Tripwires made of string and driftwood stretched from wall to wall, and the crabs were let loose to do their worst.

Finally, if the ghost reached the landing, slippery moss would send it tumbling back downstairs.

"Then we'll capture it in our nets," said Pearl, whipping them out of Fred's backpack. "Right, time to set up camp. Follow me!"

She led them to the dining room where Meg was polishing off the trifle.

"All set?" Meg asked.

Pearl nodded back. "Operation Catch a Ghost is ready! We're going to wait down here."

"I'll leave you to it then!" said Meg. And she swept off to bed. "Good luck!"

"Isn't this **thrilling,** Pirate Fredrick?!" beamed Pearl.

But Fred was too busy chewing his neckerchief to say **anything.**

Hours passed without a whisper of a ghost.

But then suddenly, as the wind rattled the windows...

"**Ghahhhhhghhhhh!**"

There it was! The awful wailing!

Fred jumped up. "C-Captain Pearl!" He prodded her awake, Edie too...

"L-l-listen."

"**Gahhhhhh-ahhh-haa!**" There it was again.

"Marvellous!" beamed Pearl. She lobbed

Fred a net then all three of them crept out to the hall. When the ghost flew downstairs in a *total* spin – they'd get it.

They waited for their jelly monster to scare the ghost off, but...

"GahhhghhaGhgaaAAAAh!"

The horrid wailing went on.

They waited for their tripwires and the crabs to do their stuff. But...

"GahhHAHGHHAGGHHH!"

Still the wailing continued.

Finally, when the moss sent nothing spinning downstairs, "Time to investigate!" whispered Pearl.

"Um—" squeaked Fred.

But Pearl was already off! It was pitch-black as they stepped on to the landing. When...

"Ahhh!"

"Fredrick!" Pearl pointed.

"The wailing. *Listen*. It's coming from inside Meg's bedroom!"

"Uh-oh!" squawked Edie.

"The g-ghost has got **Meg!**" gulped Fred.

Pearl jumped to her feet and—

"**Raaaahhh!**" burst through the door, swishing her net through the darkness.

"I've got it!" she cried as the ghostly wailing suddenly turned to a groan.

Fred switched on his torch. Under the net was...

"**Meg?!**"

Meg batted it off, glaring.

"What in Neptune's name are you **doing?**" she yelled.

"Wait! You're the ghost?" frowned Pearl.

Meg shook her head. "Don't be ridic—"

"The wailing was definitely coming from your room!" insisted Pearl.

Meg gasped. "You mean … it wasn't … a ghost? The wailing – both nights – it was … me?"

Fred nodded.

"Snorer!" squawked Edie.

"I c-can't believe I'm the mystery wailer," said Meg in dismay. "It's really *true* then."

"What's true?" asked Pearl.

Meg heaved a huge sigh. "When I worked as a cook on me old pirate ship, the captain said I ... wailed in me sleep."

She shook her head. "I insisted I did not. But the crew backed him up ... said I was regular as clockwork. Always the second Wednesday of the month. Drove them round the *bend*. I lost me job and that's how I ended up here."

"I wonder what makes you *do* it?" said Fred. "Was there anything special about those Wednesdays?"

"Well," said Meg. "We always polished

the cannons every second
Wednesday, and supper was always
... fish pie and me special trifle."

"Bingo!" nodded Pearl. "Polishing those
cannons must have worn you out and made
you snore."

"Or maybe it was the **food?**" hinted
Fred.

"The fish pie! The fish pie!" cried Pearl.

"But we had fish *every* week," frowned
Meg.

"Hmmm," said Fred. "Anything else
POP into your head?"

"Pop...?" pondered Pearl.

"Pop..." muttered Meg. And suddenly
the penny dropped.

"Well, blow me down!" she exclaimed.
"Every second Wednesday – and for the
past two nights – I've had me special t—"

"Trifle!" cut in Pearl. "Your trifle with *popping* candy. I *knew* it!"

"Pop! Pop! Pop!" squawked Edie.

"Oh no!" Meg looked *really* worried. "If Captain Swashbuckle finds out I'm a snorer, *no one* will come to me guesthouse."

Pearl rubbed her hands together. "I have a plan! Follow me." And she hurried them on to the landing.

"Now, Edie" said Pearl. "I have a *special* job for you and Fred!"

She whispered in their ears then turned to Meg.

"On the count of three you must wail **VERY** loudly ... and you, Pirate Fredrick, must be ready with the net."

"What—?" gulped Meg.

But Pearl was already counting. "One ... two ... three!"

"GAHHHAGAGAHHH!"

WUMPH! Fred brought his net down on Edie.

"**GHOST!**" roared Pearl. "Captain Swashbuckle – quick! We've caught it!"

All along the landing terrified pirates shuffled out of rooms. But then...

"Ehhh?!" Their eyes fell on *Edie* sat underneath Pearl's net.

"There was *no* ghost!" Pearl announced. "Just a parrot that snores like a tank!"

"Phew!" beamed Captain Swashbuckle. "Not that we were scared!"

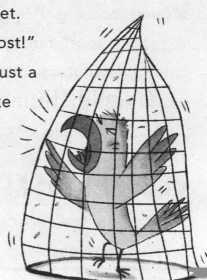

As Fred whipped the net off Edie, Pearl winked at Meg, who smiled gratefully.

"Now," said Meg. "As we're awake, who's for a midnight snack?"

The pirates piled downstairs and soon they were all scoffing sausages and beans.

"I must say, Meg," Captain Swashbuckle burped. "I'll be recommending your place to all me pirate mates. Best guesthouse around, ooo-argh!"

"Thank you!" smiled Meg. But as she wolfed down the last sausage...

"GggghhHhhahhhuuhhhh!"

–a ghostly wailing kicked off upstairs, followed by a...

CLUNK! CLUNK! CLUNK!

"Spade-at-the-Ready-Neddy!" Captain Swashbuckle gasped.

Pearl nudged Fred. "Time to go."

"Yep!" Fred whipped the toy pirate ship from his pocket.

"Touch it!" he cried, grabbing Edie.

For once Pearl did as she was told and suddenly—
WHOOSH! In a whir of bubbles, starfish and gold coins...

... they found themselves back in the Story Shop.

"Ah!" smiled Wilbur. "Safe and sound! I do hope your adventure was suitably thrilling?"

"Indeed!" nodded Pearl. She changed out of her costume and took her storybook off Wilbur.

"I shall add this to my *many* thrilling stories," she said. "Thank you, Pirate Fredrick – and Edie, old friend."

And binoculars swinging, she marched through the door, VERY NEARLY tripping over the doormat.

"Cup of tea and a snack, Fred?" Wilbur asked.

Fred chuckled. "Anything but trifle!"

Turn the page for more
pirate fun!

Can you spot the ten mistakes in this potted pirate history?

Pirates often stole their ships, renamed them and raised the pirate flag, the Jolly Rupert. The flag was black with a white skull and cross feet on it. Out at sea, pirates swarmed aboard other ships to steal their books. Food didn't keep very well on a ship and pirate biscuits were often full of spiders. A favourite pirate drink was lemonade. One of the most terrifying pirates to ever sail the seven seas was Brownbeard. His ship, the *Queen Anne's Revenge*, was armed with forty cannons. Pirates often buried their treasure to stop other pirates discovering it. They used a sat nav to find it again. Two of the most popular pirate phrases are, "Shiver me timbers!" and "Ear ear, Captain!" Pirate captains are often pictured with an eyepatch, a mouse on their shoulder and a newspaper tucked in their belt.

Answers: 1) It's the Jolly Roger not the Jolly Rupert **2)** The pirate flag has a skull and cross bones on it – not feet **3)** Pirates generally weren't looking for books to steal, they were looking for treasure **4)** Their biscuits were full of weevils **5)** Their favourite drink was grog **6)** The most famous pirate was Blackbeard! **7)** Pirates used a map to find their treasure **8)** A pirate would more likely be heard shouting "Aye aye, Captain!" **9)** Pirate captains are usually drawn with a parrot on their shoulder **10)** Pirate captains are more likely to have a cutlass than a newspaper tucked in their belt!

Who's found the treasure?
Follow the trails to find out!

Answer: It's Pearl, of course!

Tracey Corderoy is a multi-award winning author. Her first book was published in 2010 and she has since writtten over seventy books!

Her passion for nosing into other people's 'stories' began in early childhood, thanks to a set of encyclopaedias and a copy of *Cinderella*. Then one special teacher and many librarians fed Tracey more and more books. Between their pages real magic started to happen; books made her laugh, and cry and think. They made her feel that she could do things...

Tony Neal is a graphic artist and illustrator from South Leicestershire, England.

His passion for art and illustration has led him to a blooming career in children's book illustration where he now creates works for various publishing houses and clients worldwide. He has illustrated books for Usborne, Little Tiger Press, Simon & Schuster, Hachette Children's to name but a few. Tony's work is inspired by everyday life and the quirky details that surround us.

Look out for the next **Story Shop**
adventure coming soon...

When scaredy Bear stops by, Wilbur has
just the thing – a run-for-your-life
dinosaur adventure!